Little, Brown and Company

Hachette Book Group
1290 Avenue of the Americas, New York, NY 10104
Visit us at lb-kids.com

LB kids is an imprint of Little, Brown and Company.
The LB kids name and logo are trademarks of Hachette Book Group, Inc.

The publisher is not responsible for websites (or their content) that are not owned by the publisher.

First Edition: January 2015

Library of Congress Control Number: 2014934955

ISBN 978-0-316-40555-3

10 9 8 7 6 5 4 3 2 1

CW

Printed in the United States of America

Licensed By:

TRANSFORMERS RESCUE BOTS

Land Before Prime

Adapted by John Sazaklis
Based on the episode "Land Before Prime"
written by Nicole Dubuc

LITTLE, BROWN & COMPANY
LB kids

It's another regular day for the Rescue Bots and the humans patrolling Griffin Rock. Blades and Dani are scanning the skies when they come across something very strange—a pterodactyl!

"Aaaaah!" Blades cries. "Is that what I think it is?"

The creature screeches and flies toward them. Dani weaves out of its path and watches as it perches on Mount Griffin.

Dani calls Chief Burns and says, "Dad, we just saw a pterodactyl!"

"Hmm," Chief Burns replies. "Guess it doesn't know it's extinct. I'll call Doc Greene."

At the firehouse, Graham explains where the winged reptile came from. "A chain of explosions opened deep sinkholes beneath Griffin Rock," he says. "It's possible one of them reached as far down as the prehistoric caverns. There must be life within!"

The Com-Link beeps with an incoming message. It's Doc Greene. He is flying alongside the pterodactyl with a hang glider!

"This is amazing!" he exclaims. "I've never imagined seeing one of these up close!"

"When I said to observe that thing, I meant with a telescope!" Chief Burns says. "So, what's the plan?"

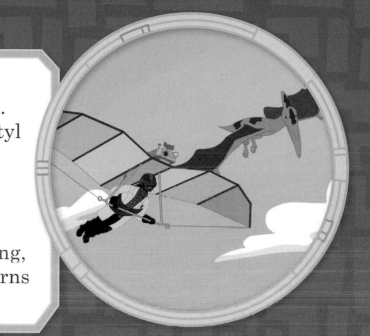

"We'll cage the pterodactyl long enough to place a tracker on her," Doc Greene says. "After she's released, we can follow her and make sure she gets home safely. My guess is that she's nesting."

The Rescue Bots follow the scientist's orders. They meet Doc Greene at Mount Griffin. Blades has a cage dangling from his winch. He drops it over the creature.

After putting a tracking device on the pterodactyl, they free her from the cage. "She's headed toward Wayward Island. That's where the subterranean rift must be located," says Graham.

"I would be happy to search for the passage myself," Doc Greene says.

"It's dangerous, Doc," Chief Burns says.

"I'll take Trex with me. What's a more logical bodyguard than a robotic dinosaur?"

Doc Greene, Trex, Kade, and Heatwave head toward Wayward Island. They soon reach the coast and pull up to the shore.

"I wonder if there really are dinosaurs on the island," Kade says.

"Only one way to find out," says Doc Greene. "We'll be back soon."

The doctor and the dino bot head deep into the dense jungle. When they reach a clearing, they see an astounding sight—real live dinosaurs!

"Great thunder lizards!" shouts Doc Greene.

A large tyrannosaur sees Doc Greene and charges at him! Trex tries to help but gets trapped by falling rocks!

While running away, Doc Greene gets lost in the jungle-like plants. He stops to catch his breath and hears a sound among the trees.

At first, he thinks Trex has escaped from the rockslide. But it's the real tyrannosaur roaring with rage!

Heatwave springs into action and sprays the dinosaur with his water blasters. "Back off, scaly!" he shouts.

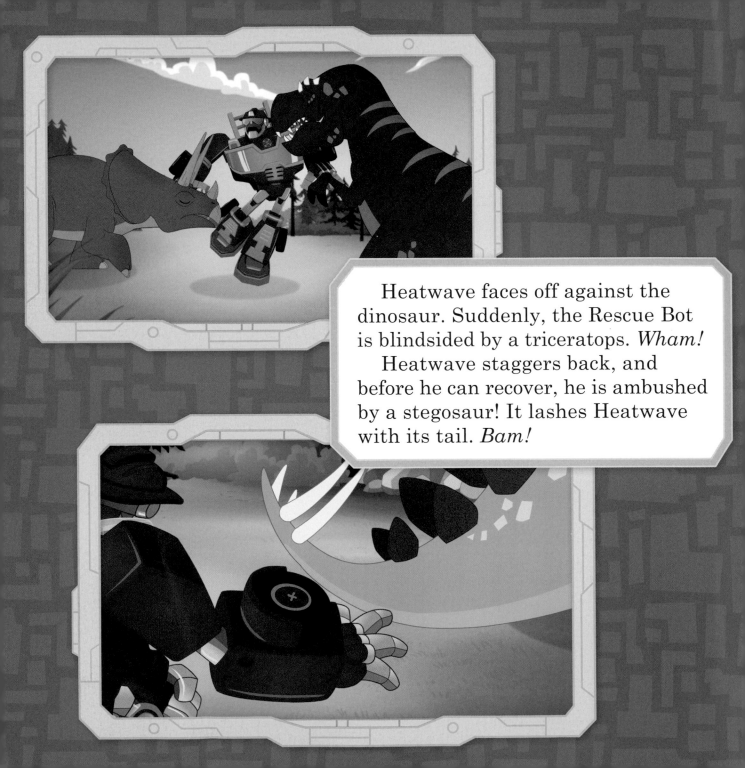

Heatwave faces off against the dinosaur. Suddenly, the Rescue Bot is blindsided by a triceratops. *Wham!*

Heatwave staggers back, and before he can recover, he is ambushed by a stegosaur! It lashes Heatwave with its tail. *Bam!*

The dinosaurs have surrounded the Autobot.

"Time to make tracks," Heatwave says. He changes into fire-truck mode. "Hop in, Doc, before those things smash me into fossil fuel!"

Doc Greene jumps into the moving vehicle, and Heatwave races back to the shore.

Meanwhile, Optimus Prime arrives at headquarters. "I heard about the subterranean passage and came to oversee the mission," he says. "Those dinosaurs could have been living underground for millions of years!"

All of a sudden, a distress call from Kade comes in. "The dinosaurs are acting up, and we're in trouble!" he says.

Optimus Prime deploys the rest of the team. "Rescue Bots, roll to the rescue!" he commands. Only he and Cody stay behind.

Once the entire team arrives at Wayward Island, Heatwave and Doc Greene lead them into the jungle.

"The dinosaurs tried to enter the passage, but a rockslide occurred," says Doc Greene. "Trex is trapped under some boulders. We have to save him and help the dinosaurs get home!"

The heroes find Trex, but as soon as they approach, they hear a terrible roar!

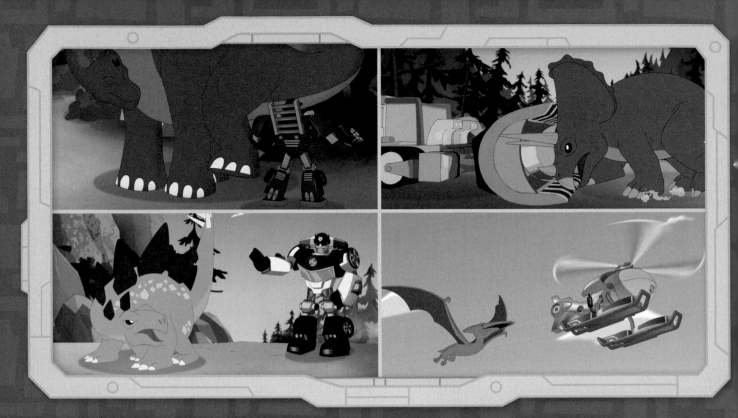

The tyrannosaur has returned, and he's brought his friends along for another fight!

"Stop! We're trying to help you!" cries Heatwave as a brachiosaur slams him into the ground. A triceratops locks its horns with Boulder, a stegosaur gets ready to slam Chase, and the pterodactyl stalks Blades.

"Fall back and regroup!" Heatwave shouts. The Rescue Bots change into vehicles and retreat from the rumble.

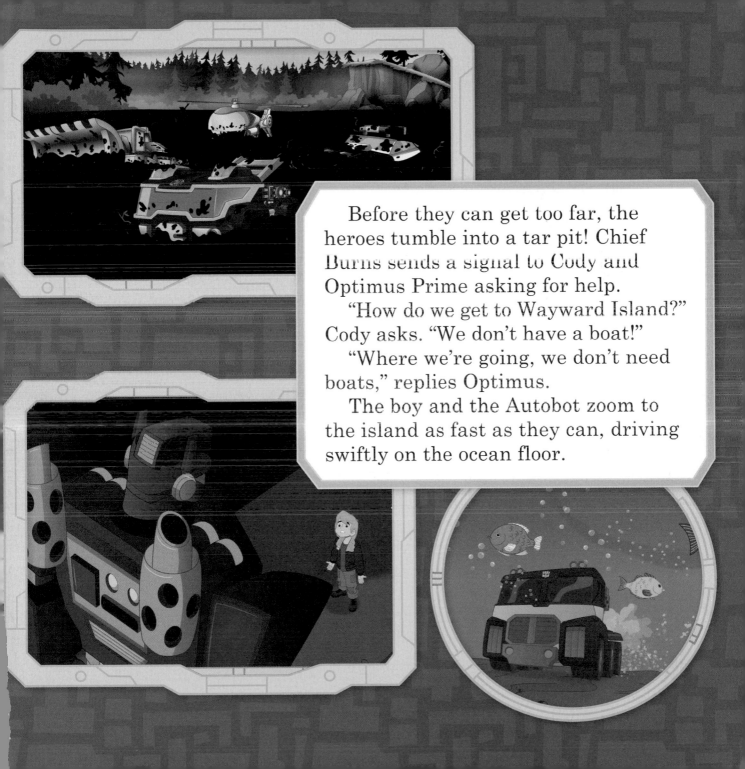

Before they can get too far, the heroes tumble into a tar pit! Chief Burns sends a signal to Cody and Optimus Prime asking for help.

"How do we get to Wayward Island?" Cody asks. "We don't have a boat!"

"Where we're going, we don't need boats," replies Optimus.

The boy and the Autobot zoom to the island as fast as they can, driving swiftly on the ocean floor.

When Cody and Optimus arrive, they find the team trapped in the tar pit, surrounded by dinosaurs.

"How can we help them if the dinos won't let us through?" Cody asks.

"These creatures view anything not a dinosaur as a threat," answers Optimus. Then, he has an idea. "Perhaps Trex can help *us*!"

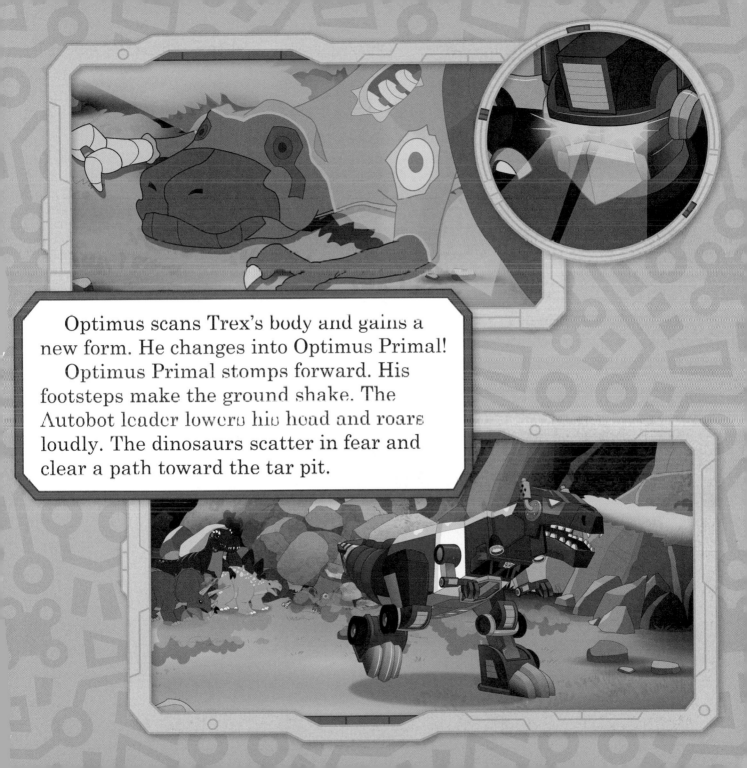

Optimus scans Trex's body and gains a new form. He changes into Optimus Primal! Optimus Primal stomps forward. His footsteps make the ground shake. The Autobot leader lowers his head and roars loudly. The dinosaurs scatter in fear and clear a path toward the tar pit.

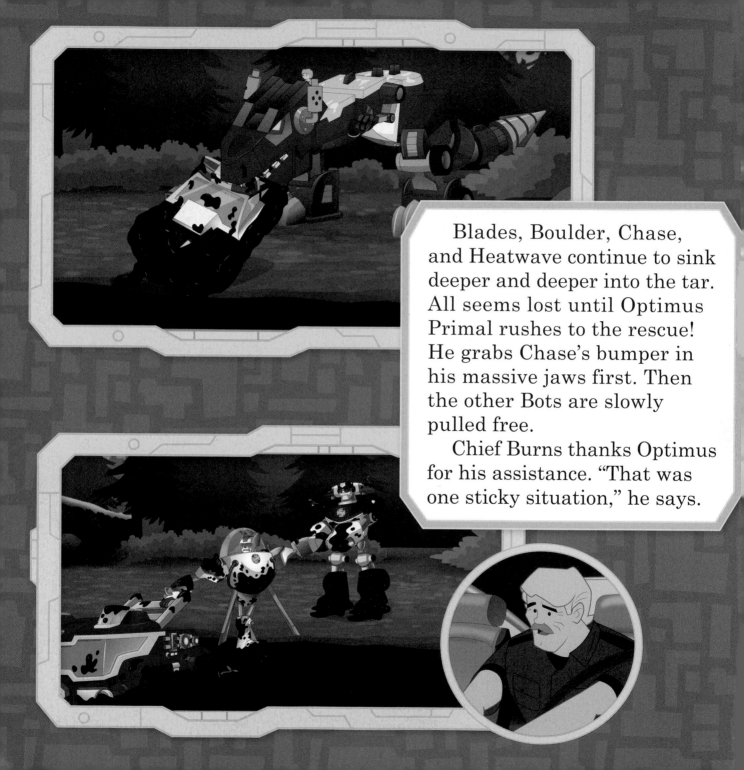

Blades, Boulder, Chase, and Heatwave continue to sink deeper and deeper into the tar. All seems lost until Optimus Primal rushes to the rescue! He grabs Chase's bumper in his massive jaws first. Then the other Bots are slowly pulled free.

Chief Burns thanks Optimus for his assistance. "That was one sticky situation," he says.

Together, the team returns to free Trex. Using his new powers, Optimus Primal unleashes a sonic roar. The massive sound waves blast the rocks into tiny pieces. Trex is free, and the underground passage is open once again!

The team then makes a startling discovery—a nest full of baby dinosaurs!

"This explains why the creatures emerged," says Optimus Primal. "They were foraging for food for their young."

"They are *so* cute!" Kade squeals. "Just look at 'em!"

"Let's seal up that crack so they can stay safe underground again," Graham says. Together, the Rescue Bots and their friends move the boulders back into place.

"Everyone to the boat," says Chief Burns when they are finished. "It's time this mission became prehistory!"